Seals of the Antarctic

Sally Cowan

Contents

Seals Living in the Antarctic

Seals are animals that live in the sea. There are many kinds of seals around the world. Several of them live in the **Antarctic**.

Four kinds of seals live on the ice and in the waters around Antarctica. They are crabeater seals, leopard seals, Ross seals and Weddell seals. Two other kinds of seals are found on islands in the Antarctic. They are fur seals and southern elephant seals.

A leopard seal swims in the sea.

Seals are excellent swimmers. They breathe air, so they have to swim up to the surface of the water to breathe. Seals also spend time on ice or land, where they rest and care for their **pups**.

Two crabeater seals rest on the ice.

What Seals Look Like

Seals have smooth heads and long, **sleek** bodies for gliding easily through the water.

Most seals are much fatter in the middle of their bodies. They have thick **blubber** that helps them keep warm in the water. They have fur on their bodies to give them extra warmth on land.

Fur seals do not have blubber. They have a thick coat of fur on their bodies to keep them warm.

a leopard seal

a crabeater seal

Seals have strong front flippers and smaller tail flippers. The flippers allow seals to swim fast and twist and turn underwater. Out of the water, most seals wriggle and drag themselves along the land. They also slide on the slippery ice.

Fur seals are different. They can walk on all four flippers on land.

A fur seal walks on all four of its flippers.

Most seals are grey or brown, with pale bellies. Weddell seals have dark patches, and leopard seals have black spots.

Seals have nostrils that close tightly to stop water getting in their noses. But they can open their mouths wide underwater to grab prey with their sharp teeth. Seals have large eyes to see well underwater. Their whiskers can sense movement in the water, which also helps them hunt for prey.

Most seals just have tiny holes for ears, but fur seals have ears with flaps to keep water out.

Fur seals have small flaps over their ears.

Seals can hear underwater and often call loudly to each other.

Many seals are between two and three metres long. Leopard seals are slightly larger. Male southern elephant seals are the largest seals in the world. They have long noses, which they can use to make roaring sounds.

Sizes of Antarctic Seals

fur seal 2 m

Ross seal 2.3 m

crabeater seal 2.5 m

Weddell seal 3 m

leopard seal 3.5 m

southern elephant seal (male) 6.5 m

A Cold Home

The Antarctic is the coldest area on Earth. The ocean and ice are the **habitat** of seals.

There are huge areas of "fast ice", which is ice that is attached to land. These areas stay frozen all year. There is sea ice, too. It floats on the sea. The amount of sea ice changes with the seasons.

Seals rest on a huge sheet of fast ice.

In summer, much of the sea ice melts. There are many cracks in the fast ice, too. Seals can always find places to breathe and **haul** themselves out of the water to rest.

Seals often rest on the sea ice.

In winter, there is more sea ice, and any cracks in the fast ice freeze over. Crabeater seals and leopard seals move to the edge of the sea ice so that they can keep on hunting in the sea. They sometimes swim to the Antarctic islands, where the weather is a little warmer.

A leopard seal swims in warmer waters.

Weddell seals stay around the fast ice for their whole lives. Their huge bodies have lots of blubber for surviving the freezing winter. They have to keep holes in the ice open so they can breathe. Every day, they scrape the ice away from the edges of the holes using their teeth.

During **blizzards**, seals often stay underwater. The water is almost the same temperature all year round, so it can be warmer than being out on the ice.

Weddell seals keep holes in the ice open so they can come up to breathe.

What Seals Eat

Antarctic seals hunt for their food in the Southern Ocean. Most seals eat **krill**, and some also eat fish, squid and prawns.

Seals spend a lot of time swimming and diving while searching for food. They sometimes dive very deep. Weddell seals can dive to 700 metres and stay underwater for about 45 minutes.

A group of Antarctic krill swim under a sheet of ice.

A Weddell seal swims under the ice.

Elephant seals dive even deeper, to over 2000 metres. They can stay underwater for more than an hour.

A southern elephant seal pokes its head out of icy water.

Crabeater seals do not eat crabs. They eat large amounts of krill every day. Crabeater seals and leopard seals have special teeth that trap the krill inside their mouths, while letting water flow out again.

Leopard seals do not only eat krill – they eat almost anything, including penguins and the pups of other kinds of seals.

This leopard seal is hunting a penguin.

Caring for Seal Pups

Some of the seals in the Antarctic give birth to their pups on the ice. Others have their pups on land. The seal mothers come out of the sea in spring. They usually have one pup.

The mother stays with her pup for up to four months, feeding it milk. The mother finally leaves her pup when it is large enough to hunt on its own.

A leopard seal mother and her pup rest on the ice.

Pups on the Ice

Crabeater seals, leopard seals, Ross seals and Weddell seals all have their pups on the ice.

Weddell seals go to the same area of fast ice every year to have their pups. The pups are born with lots of grey fur. The fur helps them stay warm on the ice. When a pup is about one week old, the mother slips into the water through a crack in the ice. She calls to the pup to encourage it to follow her. Then, she teaches her pup how to swim and dive.

A Weddell seal mother and her pup swim underneath the ice.

The male seals sometimes stay with the mothers for a little while, but they do not look after the pups.

A leopard seal mother looks after her pup.

Pups on the Islands

Some fur seals and southern elephant seals gather in large **colonies** on the Antarctic islands.

The fur seal mothers stay with their pups for about four months. During this time, the mother leaves her pup on the beach while she goes hunting in the sea close to the colony.

Fur seals have their pups on the Antarctic islands.

The elephant seal mothers stay on the beach with their pups for about a month, without eating. But the pups are not always safe in the colony. Sometimes, the male elephant seals fight each other. Pups can be crushed if they get in the way of the enormous males.

A southern elephant seal mother looks after her pup on the beach.

Surviving in the Antarctic

Seals must survive harsh weather and fierce predators in the Antarctic. Their main predator is the orca, or killer whale.

Seals, whales, fish and penguins all eat krill. Therefore, having large amounts of krill in the ocean is important for the survival of these animals.

An orca is stalking seals while they rest on the ice.

There is a serious problem for animals in the Antarctic. It is **climate change**. The Earth is getting warmer, and each year less sea ice forms in the Antarctic. Krill use the ice for shelter, and they eat **algae** that grows on the ice. If there is less sea ice, there will be less krill. There will not be enough food for all the other animals.

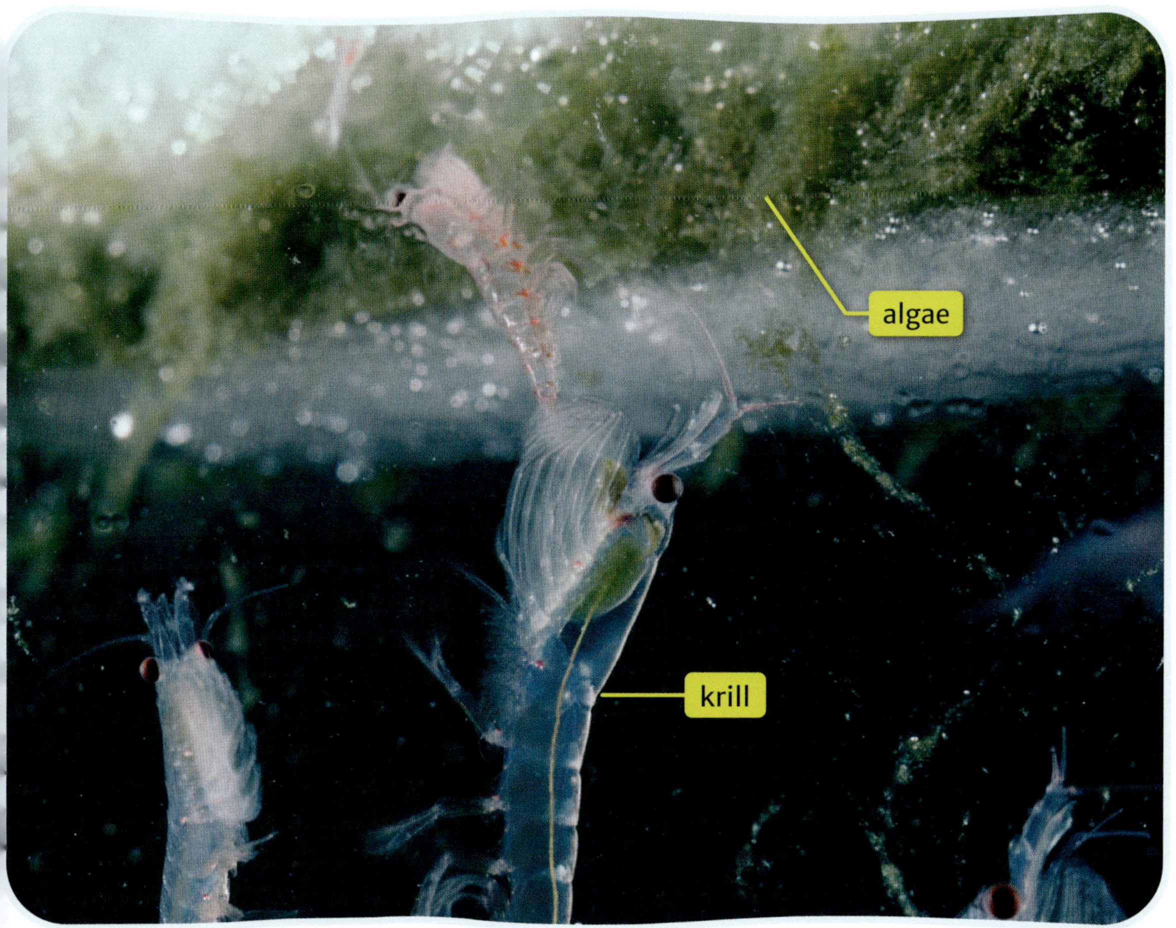

Krill feed on algae that grows on the ice.

Many people are working hard to stop climate change from getting worse. Scientists are learning more about the Antarctic and how people can help the animals that live there. Life for seals may become more difficult in the future, but they are great survivors.

Three crabeater seals rest on the ice.

Glossary

algae (*noun*) a kind of tiny plant that grows in water

Antarctic (*proper noun*) a large area around the South Pole, including the continent of Antarctica, Antarctic islands, sea and ice

blizzards (*noun*) cold winter snowstorms

blubber (*noun*) a layer of fat under the skin of marine mammals

climate change (*noun*) a change in weather patterns around the world

colonies (*noun*) large groups of animals that gather together on land

habitat (*noun*) the place where animals usually live

haul (*verb*) to pull with a lot of effort, usually something very heavy

krill (*noun*) tiny animals with shells that live in the sea

pups (*noun*) baby seals

sleek (*adjective*) smoothly shaped for fast movement

Index